foreign exchange

a mystery in poems

MEL GLENN

morrow junior books
new york

In memory of Paul L. Weiss,
a dedicated teacher

Published by Morrow Junior Books
a division of William Morrow and Company, Inc.
1350 Avenue of the Americas, New York, NY 10019
www.williammorrow.com

Printed in the United States of America.

10 9 8 7 6 5 4 3 2 1

Library of Congress Cataloging-in-Publication Data
Glenn, Mel.
Foreign exchange: a mystery in poems / Mel Glenn.
p. cm.
Summary: A series of poems reflect the thoughts of
various people—town residents young and old, teachers,
and some students visiting from the city—caught up in
the events surrounding the murder of a beautiful high
school student who had recently moved to the small
lakeside community of Hudson Landing.
ISBN 0-688-16472-2
1. Young adult poetry, American.
[1. City and town life—Poetry.   2. Murder—Poetry.
3. Prejudices—Poetry.   4. American poetry.]   I. Title.
PS3557.L447F67 1999   811'.54—dc21   98-40551   CIP AC

prologue

jolene hanks, owner, hudson hardware

To the summer people, looking for the simpler life,
Hudson Landing is always the same;
It never changes.
For them, it emerges every year under the hot sun
When sailboats and swimmers dot the lake,
And young couples from the city
Ask about real estate prices on lots just outside town.
Now things have changed forever.
Our town will be invaded by outsiders,
Caught in the glare of media attention.
Simpler times will shatter forever, like ice breaking
    up on the lake.
The old-timers at the coffee shop remember the
    old times,
When the logging trucks rolled through at all hours,
When there were three good restaurants on
    Main Street,
When people square-danced every Tuesday night in
    Veterans' Park.
I remember, most of all, the Majestic Theater—
Saturday afternoons of popcorn and two-reelers,
When we screamed at monster movies,
And Evan, my future husband, chased me down
    the aisles.
The Majestic closed thirty years ago.
Now I remember the good old days,
When *War of the Worlds* raged and Evan was too
    shy to kiss me.
The monsters have returned.
This time they're real.

john erikson, town constable

My name is John Erikson,
And I'm the local police—
Not that this town needs much policing.
There's so little for me to do
I spend more time than I should at the coffee shop,
Arguing 'bout our miserable high school football team.
The population of the town is 1,232,
But we seem to be havin' a lot of births lately.
The population rises during hunting season,
And in the summer, when city people
Come up for the cool breezes off the lake.
Major crime here consists of
A little too much drinking Saturday nights,
A few cases of shoplifting at the new supermarket,
And teenagers cruising up and down Main Street
    at night.
(We have a new curfew law that ought to cut down
    on that.)
We've got one traffic light at Main and Broad,
And often there are more bicycles than cars on
    the street.
People have time to talk to their neighbors,
    without hurrying,
Time to do their chores without being rushed by
    the clock,
Time to take a few hours off for fishing without
    feeling guilty.
We were a sleepy little town, nestled in the mountains,
But now we are fully awake, screaming bloody murder.

kristen and kwame

kristen clarke

I chase the horizon once more,
Looking for what lies over the next hill.
I seem to be driving much too fast these days,
Not slowing down for school, friends, or family.
I am in such a rush to leave this town
That I skip the landmarks of my own life,
Preferring my own company to that of people
I have known for the past six months,
Ever since my father made us move here
After he and my mom got divorced.
Oh, I know the names they call me—
Snob, Ice Princess, Tease, and worse—
But I can't hear them above the whine of the tires.
I am thirty miles out of town in a second.
I am flying with the wind, trying to catch up.
One day I'll really leave this town for good
And not limp back, ashamed, to Hudson Landing,
After nightfall.

 # kwame richards

I bury my head in my studies once more,
Looking for the answers to my next test.
I seem to be driving myself too fast these days,
Not slowing down for friends or family.
I am in such a rush to leave this city
That I skip the high points of my own life,
Preferring the company of books to that of people
I have known for years,
Ever since my family moved here.
Oh, I know the names they call me—
Oreo, White Boy, Cracker, and worse—
But I can't hear them above the music on my stereo.
I am miles out of town in my imagination.
I am flying with the wind, trying to learn everything.
One day I'll leave this city for good
And not crawl back, ignorant, to the projects
After nightfall.

kristen clarke

I was eight when I lost
The Miss Sweetie-Pie Beauty Contest.
My father tried to pick up my spirits,
As we watched the winner
Take her triumphant stroll down the runway.
I told my father I was too ugly to win anything.
"Are you crazy?" he yelled.
"There are other contests we can enter."
"I'm never gonna do this again."
"What?" he said.
"I'm never gonna do this again," I repeated.
His mouth dropped open.
I didn't know if he was gonna hit me or hug me.
Later that night he told the story to anyone
    who'd listen.
I didn't know whether to feel ashamed or proud.
We moved to another city the next month.

Song to myself:
Mirror, mirror, on the wall,
Who is the ugliest of them all?
Pick me, pick me.

kwame richards

I was eight when the fire
Gutted our basement apartment.
My father picked me up like a fumbled football,
And we all dashed out of the house.
We watched as the firemen
Sprayed water and broke windows.
I told my father I had to go back in.
"Are you crazy?" he yelled.
"It's still burning in there."
"But I gotta get something."
"What?"
"My homework," I said. "I need it for tomorrow."
His mouth dropped open.
I didn't know if he was gonna hit me or hug me.
Later that night he told that story to anybody
       who'd listen.
I didn't know whether to feel ashamed or proud.
We moved to the projects the next month.

kristen clarke

Sometimes,
I think I hear footsteps,
I think I hear whispers, *ssh ssh ssh ssh.*
I think someone is looking at me, *oo oo oo oo.*
Oh, I know the guys stare at me,
Not that I stare back.
Once I saw a guy looking at me,
And then he bumped right into a lamppost
And said, "Excuse me."
But this is different,
Strange,
Spooky,
Like an evil breeze at my back.
When I lived in the city,
I never felt any fear at all—
There were too many people around.
But out here,
When sometimes there is no one around,
I get the feeling I am not alone.
Does this sound crazy?
Do you think I'm being paranoid?

johnny nesbitt

Ms. Gardiner, I really can't take your history test.
I studied, but the truth of it is, well,
I'm sort of hung over.
I know a lot, really I do.
I know famous men from history,
Like Jim Beam and Jack Daniel.
I know geography,
Like beer from Milwaukee, vodka from Sweden.
I know math,
Like one-fifth plus one-fifth....
I know American lit,
Like Poe, Fitzgerald, and Hemingway all drank.
Can I take a makeup?
Can I do something for extra credit?
What's this test on, anyway?
The 1920s and '30s? I can do that.
People drank then, even if they weren't allowed to.
I don't feel so good, Ms. Gardiner; can I be excused?
When I drink like this, I don't remember what I did.
Maybe they should just bring back Prohibition.

melinda kurtz

Well, well, will you take a look at that?
There go Kristen and her entourage.
Sounds like a rock group, doesn't it?
How long's she been in town anyway?
I swear, nobody has the right to be that beautiful.
Nobody has the right to stop traffic like that—
As if we had any traffic to stop.
The guys all want her;
The girls all want to be like her.
When God gave out looks,
Seems she ran to the head of the line.
Not that I'm jealous, mind you.
I just wonder what there is to work on
When everything is just so perfect.
Too perfect, if you ask me.
She's gotta have a secret; everyone has one.
Where does she go in the afternoons?
Everybody's got a skeleton in her closet.
I know people who have wardrobes.
Naah, she's gotta have a secret.
Maybe she's got a secret like mine.

brian paxell

Got my first brother when I was eight.
Got my first sister when I was nine.
  Didn't know which I hated more.
Got my first dog when I was ten.
Got my first rifle when I was eleven.
  Didn't know which I loved more.
Got my first job when I was twelve.
Got my first high school report card when I
  was thirteen.
  Didn't know which I liked less.
Got my first girl when I was fourteen
Got my first truck when I was fifteen.
  Liked gettin' the girl in the truck.
Sixteen, seventeen—ain't nothin' left to get,
'Ceptin' my education, some people say.
But I figure, Who needs to get that
When I got everything else?
Maybe I'll join the army when I hit eighteen.
They might show me if there's
Anyone or anything
To get.

yvette rondeau

When Brian Paxell was through with me,
I didn't quite get it at first
And made excuses for his
Not showing up,
Or showing up too drunk to do anything.
I pretended he was still my boyfriend,
Even as I carried his baby to term,
Giving it up to Dr. Hicks, who convinced me
There was no way I could take care of my little girl.
Brian said it wasn't his;
We both knew he was lying.
I live just outside town,
Had to drop out and find work when I could.
I saw Brian the other day by his truck,
Making a move on Kristen Clarke.
He should stay away from her.
And he thought *I* was wild?
That girl's trouble waiting to happen.
I could tell by the way he looked at her
He'd never look at me again.
Oh, Brian, why are you so mean
When the only thing I ever did wrong was love you?
Maybe, before the snow starts to fall,
I can find a job in the next town over.

 # johnny nesbitt

My father used to take me fishing.
We'd get up early, just me and him,
And before the sun rose, a finger at a time,
We'd settle along the shore and drown a few worms.
Fish caught were less important than
Hours spent together, quietly,
Waiting to see who would catch the biggest one.
Sometimes he'd tell me funny stories
About his customers, especially city folks,
Who would try each summer to bargain down
    his prices.
"Watch out for Jews; they're the worst," he'd say.
"Watch out for blacks; they steal," he'd say.
Sometimes he'd tell me dirty jokes, which my
    mother hates.
But ever since they opened that new supermarket,
"The little guy always gets screwed," he always says.
I can't remember the last time we were on the lake.
My father used to take me fishing.
He doesn't have the time for it anymore.

amy sWintOn

While my friends can't wait to leave town,
I can't wait to photograph it,
Especially in the fall, when the tall trees
Dressed in reds and yellows
Bring an artist's paintbrush to the shoreline.
I want to frame the lake,
Loon by loon, tree by tree,
And freeze for the moment
Nature caught changing its seasonal clothes,
Far from my mother's gull-like cries.
Winter advisories thrill me.
Coming frost invigorates me
As I set up my tripod,
Prepared to wait all day
For the right light or the right animal
To cut across my field of vision.
I like moonlit nights too, after everyone's asleep,
The lake almost as bright as day,
The whole body of water,
Enhanced by different lenses,
Modeling just for me.

 # the dropout

You don't want to know my name.
It don't mean nothin' anyway.
I am one more application
For a job that don't exist.
I am one more number
On the unemployment line.
I am one more logger
For trees too protected.
I am one more miner
For the pits that have closed.
I got a part-time job at the Royale,
Sticking prices on cans of soup.
What's the shelf life of that?
The manager's blue-eyed daughter's
Got a cute ass.
That's all the entertainment 'round here.
Maybe she'll go out with me.
No chance of that happening.
She don't even know my name.
Nobody knows my name.
I'm nobody.

the drifter

Home is where my Harley roars,
Never resting in any one place for long.
Home falls on the highways and hills,
Crisscrossing the two-lane blacktops
That lie in the shadow of the interstates.
The small towns all look the same—
The courthouse, the plaza, Main Street,
Standing silently in frozen boredom.
The girls too look the same,
Washed-out creatures who see me
As the vehicle to escape
The windswept landscape of their loneliness.
I can easily spot the unhappy ones.
A few promises, a little weed,
That's all it takes.
"Hey, sweetheart, what's your name?
Kristen? That's a fine name.
Come over here a minute.
You want to ride on my big machine?
I can take you away from all this."

penny marsden

Kristen Clarke does not have to work.
Her father runs this damn supermarket.
She certainly doesn't have to work near me.
It's annoying how the boys line up at her register.
Kristen doesn't mind working; she enjoys it.
I have to work; I hate it.
Is it my fault I have to put in
A full shift, after school,
That makes me too tired to say I'm tired?
Is it my fault my parents had five children,
My father lost his job at the paper mill,
And we're nearly broke?
Maybe I'll just get pregnant,
Get off my feet for a while,
And become a member of the "Babyclub,"
Like a lot of other girls 'round here do.
And then go over to Dr. Hicks's office.
I try not to think of these things
As I watch Kristen flirt outrageously,
And see myself punching out prices for fresh
     corn forever.
Is she charging for the merchandise
Or giving it away for free?

kristen clarke

Oh, Daddy, you were worried?
That's so silly.
I can take care of myself.
Went out.
For a drive.
Yes, alone.
Yesterday?
Didn't do anything.
What motorcycle?
What are you talking about?
I wouldn't do anything like that.
I don't care what people told you.
They're just old gossips.
The whole town lies.
Don't you trust me?
Working?
Can't today, those kids are visiting,
And then there's the dance at the gym.
Besides, I won't work when Penny is there.
She hates me.
No, I don't know why.
I'm nice to everyone.
Oh, Daddy, you were worried?
That's so silly.

 # joe fromer

Happened like this, John.
It's about five in the morning,
Sun's comin' up, tryin' to cut its way through the fog,
Which is hanging over the water like a blanket.
I swear, nothin' is biting, I mean *nada*.
I prop up my pole, let the boat drift a bit,
Take some coffee from my thermos.
I see a heron flappin' his wings,
Taxiing 'cross the water.
I pick up my pole again, and the line is snagged,
On some marsh grass, I think; only it's not
marsh grass.
I reel in, a tire maybe? A sack of garbage?
But it's a body, a girl dressed in white,
Floating in the water like some rubber doll.
I recognize her; it's that Kristen girl, Ned
Clarke's daughter.
I struggle to get her into the boat and bring her in.
I couldn't just leave her out there, could I?
Droppin' a line into the water, I should get
The gills of a fish, not the wings of an angel.
You gonna arrest anybody soon, John?

BODY FOUND IN LAKE

Joe Fromer, a local resident out fishing early yesterday on Hudson Lake, found the body of seventeen-year-old Kristen Clarke. The girl, a senior honor student at Hudson Landing Central High School, had been the subject of a county-wide search since last night. Authorities await the results of the medical examiner's report, but unconfirmed sources indicate the popular teen may have been strangled.

Police have been questioning family and friends. Reportedly, the last person to see her alive was Kwame Richards, one of a group from Tower High School, which was participating in a student exchange program. Police will not say whether he is a suspect.

Mr. Clarke remains in seclusion. He is the manager of the recently opened Grande Royale Supermarket here in town.

This is the second recent tragedy for the town. Three years ago last February a bus carrying members of the Tower High basketball team flipped over on an icy road and tumbled down a ravine, killing three and injuring ten.

six months earlier

jason palmer

I've known the same group of kids for so long
It feels like we are one family.
To go out with any of the girls
Would seem like incest.
To fight with any of the guys
Would seem like a family feud.
    Buddy's father is town constable,
    Brian's family, out on the farm, is strict.
    Aaron's family runs the dairy farm just out of town,
    And Johnny's father runs the town store.
The five of us would be a basketball team
If any of us were good enough to play varsity.
We all hang together, waiting for something to happen.
But only boring stuff does, like tonight's town
    council meeting.
Heard that a new girl just moved to town.
Her father's the manager of the supermarket that just
    opened up.
I figure it's time for me and my friends to check
    her out.

becky beauclaire

I've known the same group of kids for so long
It feels like we are one family.
To go out with any of the guys
(Except Buddy, my one true love)
Would seem like incest.
To fight with any of the girls
Would seem like a family feud.
    Valerie's family is goin' through tough times,
    Melinda can't wait to graduate and go to the city.
    And Amy's mother is practically town supervisor.
The four of us would be a good track team
If any of us were good enough to run varsity.
We all hang together, waitin' for something to happen.
But only boring stuff does, like tonight's town
    council meeting.
Heard that a new girl just moved to town.
Her father's the manager of the supermarket that just
    opened up.
I figure it's time for me and my friends to check
    her out.

oliver nesbitt, town board member no. 1

Well, I think it's a bad idea.
Who wants *them* to come to our pretty town?
I mean, that's the reason
Most of us moved up north, right?
You let one of them see how nice it is,
They'll tell their parents and all their relatives,
And before you know it, we'll be invaded by them.
And I would never let my son go down to the city
As part of some silly exchange group.
If our schoolchildren want to see the world,
Let them use the Internet.
And here's another thing:
These kids smoke, drink,
And do other things
I can't describe in mixed company.
It's a bad idea any way you look at it.
I vote no.

# bill paxell, town board member no. 2

My friend Ollie, you should stay in your store on
    Main Street.
You make the best sandwiches
And wear the worst hat in the county.
The board should take up a collection
To replace that ratty red hunting cap you wear.
And how come you didn't bring any subs over?
We could sure use them now.
But seriously, Ollie, you should know
You can't stop progress.
If there is change, you're against it.
You voted against the folk festival.
You voted against the new supermarket.
Shoot, you would have voted against the lake
If it weren't here before you were born.
What are you afraid of?
They're going to wreck your place?
Not hardly.
Other communities have done similar exchanges,
And from what I hear they were wonderful experiences.
Ollie, there shouldn't be a sign on your shelf that says
WHITE BREAD ONLY.
I vote yes.

edith fromer, town board member no. 3

Whether we like it or not,
There will always be a terrible connection
Between Tower and Hudson High,
A terrible tie that has knotted us together.
Have you forgotten the faces of the injured?
Have you forgotten the pain of the parents?
Have you forgotten the memorial service in the rain?
How many people did you hug that awful weekend?
When kids die, there is not one small,
    isolated community
But a city of sorrow, a town of trouble.
In a big city, deaths might slip back into oblivion.
But here, in a small town, each thread,
Each life, is to be cherished.
We remember those poor children.
Of course I vote yes.

dr. adolphus hicks,
town board member no. 4

Let's be practical here, folks.
Hudson doesn't have enough resources, financial
    or otherwise,
To put these teenagers up,
Now that the summer people have gone.
In case you don't remember our treasurer's report,
We are practically drowning in debt,
Barely treading water with summer revenue.
One day our town might be strong enough
To hold its head fiscally abovewater.
One day families might flock to our town.
I have a plan, but I am not in a position
To announce it to you at this time.
May I remind you that half of our population
Receives public assistance.
Half of them blow their money at Finnegan's Bar.
Half of our graduates—if they graduate—
Can't wait to leave Hudson Landing.
I respectfully submit that we don't need the expense;
We have to take care of our own house first
Before we show it off to the world.
I vote no.

albert goodson, town board member no. 5

I must respectfully disagree with the good doctor.
True, our community may be
Hard-pressed at the moment.
But I say education is more than dollars and cents,
More than what is seen on cable TV.
Many of our students have never been out of
    Hudson Landing.
Many of them are scared of city people.
I say let us stretch out our hands
And welcome them with open arms.
Let us show them that hospitality is not a lost art.
What are we if we close our hearts to new experiences?
What are we if we only live our lives in small circles?
We may be a small town;
We don't have to be small in spirit.
I vote yes.

Therefore, by a vote of three to two,
The motion is carried.

Any new business, folks?
If not, we stand adjourned.

 # oliver nesbitt,

Before we adjourn for the evening,
I would like to go on record
To say I think Town Constable Erikson
Deserves the highest praise
For keeping our teenagers off the streets at night.
You know, when we passed the curfew law last year,
There were many who objected,
Those civil liberty guys from the state capital,
A few troublemakers and malcontents,
And a handful of teenagers who thought
They could go anywhere, do anything they wanted.
Well, we showed them, didn't we?
Our stores are safe,
Our families sleep well at night,
And the number of petty crimes has dropped
    way down.
Our sincere thanks go to TC Erikson,
A most responsible keeper of the peace.
He has kept us out of harm's way.

albert goodson, town board member no. 5

Duly noted, Oliver.
Good night, lady and gentlemen.

 # stereotypes I

Country kids?
They milk cows,
Or tip 'em over.
They eat grass,
Or smoke it.
They marry their sisters,
Or if they're unavailable,
Their cousins will do.
They listen to twangy music
By groups like Country McDonald and the Inbreds.
They chase pigs;
Then they eat 'em.
They don't wear shoes.
They have dogs named Duke.
They have fathers named Duke.
They have broken-down refrigerators on the front lawn
And broken-down pickups in the backyard.
Sure, I want to go to the country
And tell them hicks how city kids live.

stereotypes II

City kids?
They rob people,
Or kill 'em.
They smoke grass,
Or sell it.
They beat up their sisters,
Or if they're unavailable,
Their cousins will do.
They listen to hip-hop music
By groups like LL Mojo and the Hoods.
They run from the "pigs,"
Or shoot at 'em.
They wear combat boots.
They have dogs that bite people.
They have relatives that do the same.
They have garbage spilled on their front steps
And stolen merchandise hidden in the back.
Sure, I want to go to the city
And tell those burnt-out losers how real kids live.

stereotypes III

 **the city**   **the country**

the city	the country
Black	White
Brown	White
Yellow	White
Red	White
Tan	White
Bronze	White
Burnt sienna	White
Olive	White
Ebony	White
Sepia	White
Umber	White
Mahogany	White
Café au lait	White
Ocher	White
Copper	White

henry maddox, pastor,
new deliverance church

"God loves a cheerful giver."
So it is written in the Second Corinthians.
And I am sure that the good people of Hudson Landing
Would happily give more, if they could,
But we are a poor town in a poorer county.
Oh, we donate what we can at Christmastime,
And the needy never go hungry at Thanksgiving,
But what will replenish our souls,
Who will replenish our pockets,
All the other days of the year?
I am the shepherd of a thinning flock,
The old rapidly advancing
To the threshold of Judgment Day,
The young rapidly descending
Into the maelstrom of immorality.
I am the pastor of a part-time parish,
The owner of the town's video store,
The driver of the high school bus
(Where I hear language that is hardly celestial).
A man of the cloth
Shouldn't have to work in pieces.
He should be made of whole cloth.

# oliver nesbitt, town board member no. 1

Attention, shoppers:
Have your purchases in one hand
And your plastic in another.
Please try to keep the lines moving.
Emergency! Emergency!
Shopping cart gridlock in Aisle Five.
Use alternate routes,
And follow the detour signs.
Thank you for your cooperation.
Some additional announcements:
We are open late for your shopping convenience.
We have the best merchandise in town.
So stop, shop, and save at the Town Store.
We're never too busy to help you.
   Who am I kidding?
   My store's a tomb.
   The new Grande Royale is killing me,
   Chopping me up into little packaged pieces.
   I've got to do something quick,
   Or I'm bound to be devoured
   Wholesale.

hicks manor

I sit just north of town,
Three floors of gray and blue clapboard,
And at Halloween people say ghosts fly about me.
Long ago I served as a depot stop
On the Underground Railroad.
After that Dr. Hicks's grandmother turned me into
A lodging house for gentlemen
Up from Albany who wished to escape the city's heat.
Doc owns me now, fixed me up,
And turned me into a clinic.
It's a good thing, as I'm the closest
The town has to a regular hospital.
Bones set, babies born,
Accidental gunshot wounds treated during
    hunting season:
That's what he gets, mostly,
And a few other things I can't talk about now.
Doc is getting on in years.
The clinic will probably close when he's gone,
Because a new doctor would never come
And live way up here in the wilderness.
I sit just north of town,
And when the wind swirls,
You can hear me breathing.

frank and marilyn langer

Honey, I know you're tired.
We've been on the road a long time,
But we're almost there.
Close your eyes, and when you wake up,
I promise you we'll be in Hudson Landing.
Just let me check the map again, okay?
Didn't Dr. Hicks tell us to come right away?
Didn't he sound warm and comforting?
Yes, I have the money.
Yes, we'll be there by midnight.
Don't worry about a thing.
I know we've been disappointed before,
Trusting this ad here and that lawyer there.
And sometimes last-minute changes of mind
Have sent us to the depths of despair.
But I have a good feeling in my heart tonight.
This time I know everything's going to work out right.
We're almost there; what's another hour
When we've waited five years?
So close your eyes, honey, you can close your eyes,
Because when you wake up, we're going to be a
    real family,
Picking up our package marked "Special Delivery."

dr. adolphus hicks,

town board member no. 4

I walk the streets at night,
My own medicine unable to provide peace.
Do you want to know why?
My wife ran off years ago, saying
Hudson Landing was too small for her big dreams.
My son ran off too,
Shooting the money I gave him up his arm.
Now I minister to a dying town.
I have a prescription
That will cure the town's ills,
But I can't tell you what it is.
The course of treatment is too radical
For the likes of the general establishment.
But the young people know;
They whisper it among themselves
And walk with me late at night back to my office.

alan ziegel, teacher, tower high school

All those wishing to spend a weekend in Hudson Landing, a small town upstate, are invited to a meeting this Thursday in the school's auditorium after eighth period. Just bring your enthusiasm and leave your stereotypes at the door. Refreshments will be served.

annie gardiner, teacher, hudson landing central high school

All those wishing to host a teenager from Tower High, a big-city high school, are invited to a meeting this Thursday in the school's auditorium after eighth period. Just bring your enthusiasm and leave your stereotypes at the door. Refreshments will be served.

harlan jones,

editor, *hudson valley sentinel*

Editorial

At last week's town council meeting, we noted with interest how the board gives with one hand and takes with the other, thereby sending mixed messages to the community, especially our town's teenagers.

On the positive side, the board has decided to allow a group of city teens to come and visit our fair and small town. As Al Goodson, a respected board member, said, "Education is more than dollars and cents," and "Hospitality is not a lost art." Teenagers, especially in a town that provides only minimal activities for them, need to see a world full of magic and excitement.

On the negative side, we have long argued that our curfew ordinance is unworkable, unenforceable, and un-American. You don't get results using authoritarian tactics. Instead of telling our teenagers, "Go home; stay out of sight," give them places to go, something to do.

That's why we applaud the actions of the board and welcome the students of Tower High School to our town. We have much to show and tell them. We hope it will be a weekend they never forget.

city guests, country hosts

alan ziegel, teacher, tower high school

I am *not* burning out,
Only lightly toasting.
I teach social studies at Tower,
Not the most exciting subject
For students, who are, shall we say,
Geographically challenged.
They don't know
Australia from Austria,
Canada from Kentucky,
Nome from Rome.
Their world is defined by
Their Walkmans clamped to their ears,
The parameters of their neighborhoods,
And the unshakable belief
That world history began with their births.
Their highest goal is "to chill"—
Frostbite of the mind.
Their biggest embarrassment?
To appear uncool.
I shall not go gently into retirement.
I shall not give up.
Thus my northern adventure.

annie gardiner, teacher,
hudson landing central high school

I just got tenure
And can't wait to get back to my classroom.
I teach social studies at Hudson,
The most exciting subject
For students, who lie, shall we say,
At the threshold of an exciting world.
They will learn
Paris from Pittsburgh,
Asia from Africa,
Venice from Venezuela.
Unfortunately their world is defined by
The distance to the county line,
The wicked winter that keeps them inside,
And the unshakable belief
That their future is limited by dead-end jobs.
Their highest goal?
To be popular.
The biggest embarrassment?
To appear uncool.
I shall go into my classroom.
I shall show my students there is life beyond Hudson.
This is my northern adventure.

Just talk into the camcorder, Kwame.
Say anything you like; it won't bite you.
It's your big moment.
You don't know what to say?
Aw, come on.
Usually in class I can't shut you up.
You go on a mile a minute.
Look, what would you like the Palmers to know
    about you?
Something you didn't write in your letter to them.
You still don't know what to say?
Hey, being cool doesn't mean
You have to be silent.
This trip might change your whole life.
You never know.
Ever see a real cow?
So step up to the mike, Kwame,
And say something.
The world awaits your words.

annie gardiner, teacher,
hudson landing central high school

Let's Go, Hornets, Let's Go!
Friday night football,
Social event of the week.
Mothers pray their sons don't get hurt,
Mothers remember when they met their husbands.
Hold That Line!
Friday night football,
Topic for Saturday's argument at the coffee shop.
Fathers pray their sons score touchdowns,
Fathers remember when they met their wives.
Third and Long!
Friday night football.
Time-outs and halftime let single men
Check out single women in the stands
And cheerleaders on the sly.
Defense!
Friday night football.
Team looks stronger this year.
Stale pretzels and raw corn dogs,
What am I doing here?
Let's Go, Hornets, Let's Go!

kwame richards

From the window in my building, high up,
The moon hangs so low I swear
I can reach out and grab it.
People think just because I come from the projects
My future's gonna be shooting hoops or dealing drugs.
People don't know anything.
My mama always worked,
Even though she didn't bring home much.
My mama always made sure
We did our homework, went to church,
And treated people with respect.
If someone's up front with me,
I'm up front with them.
I'm not saying I'm gonna make a million dollars.
I'm not saying I'm gonna be world-famous,
But I am saying, with God's help,
I'm gonna grab the goodies of the world
And stick them in my pocket.
I'm gonna go places, you'll see,
But I'm always gonna remember
The view from my window, high up.

jason palmer

Kwame?
What kind of name is that?
He's black, ain't he?
Not that there's anything wrong with that.
But up here he'll stand out,
Well, like a black thumb.
I know I agreed to this exchange,
But I'm having second thoughts.
I thought I'd be getting someone white.
What can we talk about?
I can tell him I like hunting,
But being from the city,
He probably knows all about guns.
I can tell him I'm in the school band,
But being from the city,
He probably likes a different kind of music.
My parents wonder if he'll fit in.
I can tell they were less than thrilled
About Kwame being black and all.
Not that there's anything wrong with that.

anthony la blanca

I'll score in the NBA;
I'll punt in the NFL;
I'll putt in the PGA;
I'll pin in the WWF;
I'll save in the NHL;
I'll hit in the AL;
I'll bunt in the NL;
I'll ride in the NYRA;
I'll strike in the PBA;
I'll kick in the MLS;
And I'll drive on the NASCAR circuit.

I'll do all this
If reality
Ever catches up
With my dreams.

buddy erikson

When I was ten,
My father said it was time.
"Time for what?" I asked.
"Time to be a man," he replied.
Which meant
Getting up early for duck season,
Getting up early for deer season,
Getting up early for fishing season.
Which meant
Standing in the rough grass,
Standing in the dark woods,
Standing in the cold water.
I told my father
I'd rather sleep than get up,
Lie down than stand up.
"Besides, I really don't like killing animals," I said.
"It's gonna be some time before you're a man," he said.

tommy la blanca

My mother put us in the same clothes—
Same haircut, same stroller.
People who thought they was seein' double
Said the same stupid stuff over and over again.
"Oh, they look so cute."
"They'll be friends for life."
"Maybe they'll meet a set of twins."
Screw that.
The more I try to be different,
The more we're the same.
We eat left-handed; we throw right-handed.
We have the same average in school—low.
We like the same kinds of girls.
You wanna know the truth?
I can't stand Anthony.
He's mean; he's loud; he's lazy.
He reminds me too much of myself.
I wanted to go on this trip alone
So I could see what it's like
To stand in the sun
Without his freakin' shadow behind me.

brian paxell

I love the smell of manure in the morning.
I love getting up early on cold autumn days,
Putting on my sweats and running for half an hour
Till Mom calls out that the pancakes are ready.
Our family eats breakfast and supper together,
Every day, every night, every day and night of the year.
My brother reminds me I promised he could use my
   baseball glove.
My sister reminds me I promised to pick her up
   after practice.
And my dad, who is on the town board,
Reminds me not to forget my homework.
My mother reminds me of my chores
And to quit daydreaming so much.
But I can't help dreaming about Kristen Clarke.
Anytime, day or night.
My mom reminds me this is the day
We host a teenager from the city
And that we should all mind our manners
So as to make a good impression.
I tell her not to worry;
We're the perfect A-one American family.
We're all so wonderful and good and perfect that
One sweet day I just might remind myself
To take the rifle Dad got me for Christmas,
Climb the roof of our very nice house,
And perfectly pick them all off, one by one.

lolita rosenbaum

It's been a bad week.
My best friend, who's a guy, started hitting on me.
Who needs that complication?
My mother found my birth control pills in my
　　book bag.
I tried to tell her they were a new kind of mint.
My English teacher gave a pop quiz on *Walden,*
And I didn't even crack open the book yet.
This trip upstate is exactly what I need now.
I'll smoke a little grass,
Commune with the cows,
And find peace and harmony
While gazing at the broad side of a barn.
I've got to get away from all the pressure of
College applications, boring teachers, and
　　nagging parents.
I've got to find my own space,
Even if it's the north forty.
I wonder, did Thoreau ever have to take the SATs?

valerie van garp

In the living room,	we will welcome my guest from the city, Lolita Rosenbaum.
In the dining room,	we will serve her barbecued beef and fresh corn.
In the guest room,	we will show her how to set the electric blanket on toasty.
In the bathroom,	we will point out which fresh towel is hers.
In the garden,	we will sit on wooden slat chairs, drink lemonade while fireflies dance.
On the porch,	we will turn off the light and smile our good-nights.

Then, in the cricket-chirping darkness,
I'll hear my parents' whispered epithets,
Mapping the borders of their imminent separation,
Carving up the acreage of the family estate.
But dividing up the property will have to wait
    for a while.
Divorce is not a spectator sport, even for
    honored guests.

stella church

I'm glad I'm away on this trip,
So I can think about the bomb
My parents just dropped on me.
I can't believe it.
My mother and father
Called me into the living room
And announced with grinning faces
That I was going to have a little sister.
How did I feel about it?
How the hell should I know?
What were they doing?
(I know the answer to that.)
What were they thinking?
(I don't have the answer to that.)
I need some time to sort out
How I feel about this.
Will it be nice to have a sister?
Will I have to give up my room?
Will I love or hate her?
I don't know.
All I know right now is
I don't want to hear the word *pregnant*
For the next few days.

melinda kurtz

I hate the cold;
I hate the heat;
I hate the town and everyone in it.
I hate my classmates;
I hate my teachers;
I hate my school and everyone in it.
But most of all, I hate Kristen.
I hate her face;
I hate her body;
I hate everything about her.
She glides like a swan;
I waddle like a duck.
She sings like a bird;
I croak like a frog.
She dresses like a princess;
I dress like a slob.
I hate her.
What I really want to know is:
How can I bring my baby into the world
When there is so much hate?
Maybe my baby will look like Kristen.

cookie maldonado

Is the camera on?
If you want to know the truth,
My real name is Lourdes Leatrice Rosalina Maldonado,
Too long to write on a name tag pinned to my
    bakery uniform,
So everyone just calls me Cookie. Cute, you think?
When my friends found out I wouldn't give them
    free samples,
They had other names for me I won't tell you about.
That's because my mama taught me how to be a lady.
I go to church; I save my money; I'm a good girl.
I'm the one putting away bread for college.
I'm the one with the dough.
I'm the cookie who dreams of being a radiologist.
Let my friends hang out or watch the Spanish soaps;
I'm getting out of this city.
I paid for this trip upstate.
I'm saving up for an away college.
I can't wait to meet Kristen Clarke and her family.
That's the family I'm staying with.
I'm bringing them a special box of pastries.
I hope they like them,
And me.
Would you like a cookie from Cookie, Mr. Ziegel?

kristen clarke

There's not much to do in Hudson Landing
But walk down country roads
With my guitar in hand and
Say hello to people
Who, after you pass by,
Whisper something nasty about you.
But there's so much to do in the city,
Like walk down crowded streets
With my guitar in hand and
Not say hello to people
Who, after you pass by,
Shout something obscene at you.
One day, after I graduate,
I'll go to the city
With my guitar in hand and
Knock on the front doors of
Coffeehouses and clubs
And sing about the people
Who, after you pass by,
Whisper, talk, and shout
Their fragile, sad messages to the world.

angie perry

Most people in school don't know
I live in a group home.
Been here for three years;
No friends have ever been over.
My father walked out on my mother,
And my mother walked out into traffic.
I don't even blame the guy who hit her.
None of my relatives wanted me,
So I'm stuck here, at least till I'm eighteen.
I take two buses to school, and two back.
Then there are my chores:
I do the laundry;
I do the dishes;
I clean the toilets;
I clean my room;
I mop the floors;
I shop for food.
By the time I'm finished,
I'm too tired to do my homework.
You don't know what trade-offs I made
To go on this here trip.
One day I'm gonna leave this place
And find a real family of my own.

 # becky beauclaire

Nothin' to do in this town
But watch your body grow fat.
(Too many shakes at the DQ,
Too many shakes in the back of a van.)
Or watch your body grow thin.
(Too many pills, abuse them,
Too many meals, then lose them.)
Nothin' to do, it seems, but get pregnant.
It's a regular growth industry 'round here.
I personally know two girls who are knocked up,
And three others who'd like to be.
Maybe I'll have one myself—
That is, if I can find anyone who is not drunk
    or stoned.
Makin' babies sure don't take a lot of time.
Hell, what do you do after five seconds?
There's got to be more to life than screwin' around.

michael perrin

My mother knocks on my door,
Chanting prayers for the dead,
Her way of objecting
To my home-to-school, school-to-home life.
"You need a passion or purpose," she says.
"I'm not going to find it in my math class."
"You need to discover a larger world," she adds.
"I got cable," I reply.
"You need to make a connection on a higher plane."
"Before breakfast?" I ask.
My mother lived on a commune years ago,
Before surrendering to electric lights and indoor
    plumbing.
"You going on that trip with your teacher?"
"Thinking about it," I say.
"Do it," she says with vehemence.
"If you don't climb aboard that bus,
You will never know where the road will take you."

aaron loudermilk

Figured on droppin' outta school
And headin' for the coast, any coast,
But my father told me I do that
I ain't gettin' any part of his farm.
Besides, he'd come back from the grave,
Find me, and whip my ass.
He told me a warm classroom's
A lot better than a cold barn,
And if I had any sense at all
(Somethin' he doubts I have in large supply),
I better do all my learnin' now
'Cause I sure ain't gonna have the time to do it
     later on.
"But you're smart enough to hook up the machines,"
     he says.
I slammed the door then and headed toward school,
Where Ms. Gardiner asked if I got room to take in
A young visitor from the city, an exchange program,
     she said.
I like Ms. Gardiner, so I told her,
"Sure, ma'am. There's only my father and me
And a whole lotta cows."

david khalil

When we lived in the islands
After moving there from Pakistan,
Papa used to take me down to the small clinic
Where, amid broken bones and bloodstained bandages,
He toiled fifteen hours a day.
"David, my son, one day this will be yours," he joked.
When we came to America,
Papa did not take me down to the emergency wards
Where, amid shootings and stabbings,
He toiled double shifts.
"David, my son, you should choose another profession,"
    he said.
"No, Papa, I want to be a doctor," I said.
He patted my head and said, "We'll see."
Last year two holdup men shot my father dead
As he finished his shift at six A.M.
"They probably thought he was carrying drugs," the
    police said.
My mother cries when I tell her I still want to
    be a doctor.
"Like you, Papa," I say to myself, alone at night.
Maybe then I can heal the hole in my heart.

 # johnny nesbitt

My parents split up 'bout three years ago.
I'm sorta used to it,
But it's kinda hard on my little brother, Petey.
My mother works for Hudson Realty
While my father owns the Town Store,
Which sits across from her office.
They rarely speak to each other now,
'Ceptin' when my mother says she needs more money.
My father always drank; now he drinks more.
I never drank; now I drink a bit.
My friends said I should go over to Saratoga
And sit in on some AA meetings.
I did once and was shocked to discover my father there.
It's the first thing we've done together in years.

katie fung

That's my mother;
I'd know her beep anywhere.
She worries I'll get kidnapped by aliens.
She worries I'll get mugged or raped.
Not here in the park,
With Jansports littering the ground like soft rocks.
Not here in the park,
With my crew watching out for me.
We just chill here, talk about God, sex, and stuff.
Marijuana helps me forget what my parents want
    from me.
Beer helps me forget the forty-two on my math test.
Yeah, I know it's beeping again.
Screw it, ain't going home for supper anyhow,
Just need some fries from Mickey D's to carry me.
I turned off my beeper.
Who needs electronic nagging?
Maybe my mother will get the signal—
I'm busy.
Going on this trip with Mr. Ziegel tomorrow.
Just let my mother try to reach me
There.

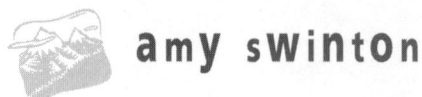 # amy swinton

That's my mother;
I'd know her voice anywhere.
She worries I'll run off to the city.
She worries I'll elope with my boyfriend.
Not here at the Dairy Queen,
With notebooks tossed on the tables like hard napkins.
Not here at the Dairy Queen,
With my friends watching out for me.
We just chill here, talk about God, sex, and stuff.
Marijuana helps me forget what my mother wants
    from me.
Beer helps me forget the twenty-four on my
    Spanish test.
Yeah, I know she's calling again.
Screw it, ain't going home for supper anyhow.
Just need some shakes from the DQ to fill me up.
I'm just going to ignore her.
Who needs amplified nagging?
Maybe my mother will get the hint—
I'm busy.
Getting a guest from the city tomorrow,
    Ms. Gardiner says.
My mother will have no time to reach me
Then.

annie gardiner, teacher,
hudson landing central high school

Do not go to Italy, my friends warned me.
The men there might be romantic,
Their eyes may shine like moonlight,
Their promises will sparkle in the Trevi Fountain.
They'll sing you the music of Milan,
The virtues of Venice,
The azure allure of the Adriatic.
They will steal your heart and lire
And leave you,
Forlorn,
Waiting in front of American Express.
And because I did not want to be disappointed in love,
I took a vacation bus ride to Cape Cod instead.
I looked out over the sand dunes and wished
I were in Florence, a tall, handsome gentleman by
     my side.
He took my hand and wondered if he was not being
     too bold.
He kissed my neck, all the while apologizing profusely.
There, with the sand in my eyes and wind in my hair,
I wish I had given my dream lover more to
     apologize for.

# lucille swintOn, parents' commmittee

The students from Tower will have a good time,
    I guarantee it.
Every second of their visit has been planned
    to perfection.
Every detail of their time here has been accounted for.
There will be activities galore, no idle moments at all.
We may be a small town, but that doesn't mean
    we're hicks.
Why, our Main Street has anything you want—
    and more.
There's the town restaurant,
    the town bank,
    the town church,
    the town store,
    the town pharmacy,
    the town real estate office,
    the town beauty salon,
    the town laundry,
    the town video store,
    the town post office,
And do not forget the new Grande Royale Supermarket.
Why go anyplace else?
Everything's right here.
Let teenagers choose what they want to do?
That's not a good idea.
Too many choices confuse people.

hudson valley sentinel
chamber of commerce insert

Antiques and Christmas Shop
Mabel Carter, prop.

Pottery, Toys, Quilts, Coins, Stamps, Postcards, Coke and Pepsi Items, Sheet Music, Decoys, Trains, Tobacco Tins
Main St.

The Breakfast Stop
Hot Coffee,
Good Talk,
Country Biscuits
Main St.

Country Consignment Auction
Farm Equipment, Stoves, Harnesses, Old Furniture
Off Davey Hill Rd.

Little Kate's
Fresh Produce • Lettuce
Corn • Cabbage • Peppers
OPP. TOWN BANK

TOWN STORE
Oliver Nesbitt, prop.
General Merchandise
Sales Daily
Main St.

Gas and Go
All Auto Repairs
Ask for Hank
Hill St.

Grand Royale Supermarket
Ned Clarke, Manager
WEEKLY SPECIALS
Super **low** prices
Come in for *free gifts*
Broad St.

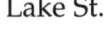

Hudson Hardware
Jolene Hanks, prop.
"You don't find it here,
It hasn't been made yet."
Lake St.

first contact

kristen clarke

When my boyfriend and me make love
In the front seat of his pickup truck,
We both take off our watches
And put them in the glove compartment
  for safekeeping.
Sometimes the steering wheel gets in the way,
But we manage to work around it.
Sometimes the upholstery sticks to our skin,
But we manage not to worry 'bout that too much.
I love the feel of his hands on my body.
I love the feeling of my body under his.
Then, there is no school time, no work time, nothin',
Just the slow time of melting into each other's arms.
He may be the boyfriend of the month, of the week,
Hell, even of the moment, I couldn't care less.
We moved to Hudson from the city less than a year ago.
I swear, my parents kept me on a leash there;
Here my father gives me a lot more freedom.
The country is safer, he claims.
I gotta make up for lost time.
Wonder where that city high school bus is.
They said five-thirty on the dot.
Maybe there'll be a couple of cute guys on it.

 # cookie maldonado

I think I see her!
I think I see her!
It must be Kristen.
Look at the sign she's holding:
WELCOME LOURDES
Hey, that's for me, *muchachos*.
My God, look how blond she is,
Her hair is practically white.
Hey, look at the school behind her.
It's all on one floor.
Look at the green fields.
I didn't know the school was in a park.
Hey, Mr. Bus Driver, let me off now!
Kristen, it's me, Lourdes.
You can call me Cookie, everyone does.
I'm so glad to be here.
Is this your family?
I brought you something.
It's from the bakeshop where I work.
Would anybody like a cookie?

aaron loudermilk

My father and I have never talked much,
And when I told him I wanted no part of his farm,
He just pointed to the door and told me to get out.
"You think you can make a living?
Go on and find out" was all he said.
So I packed my bag and left his farm for the city,
Where I soon found there was nothing I could do
'Cept make minimum wage.
Pride kept me in the city longer than I wanted,
And when I finally came back home,
I thought he would rub it in my face forever.
But he just put his arm around my shoulder and said,
"The cows need milking, son."
That was 'bout a year ago.
He never asked me what happened in the city,
Why I came back, or what I had in mind for the future.
We go about our business,
Tend to the cows and the machinery,
And let life take care of itself,
Without much talking.
Michael, the kid from the city, is coming here soon.
I'd like to show him my farm.

 # michael perrin

Mr. Ziegel, I'm having second thoughts about this trip.
Who wants to see a bunch of dopey horses?
Who wants to go on a corny hayride?
I'd rather stay in my room and play video games
And use weapons of mass destruction to wipe out
    the universe,
Or go out with my friends and just chill,
Or go to the park and hang out, smoke some weed,
Or go to the cemetery and sit on some gravestones,
Or I don't know, just walk up and down the block.
If you look at it, life's kinda boring.
You wait and wait for something to happen,
And something never does.
Where is my Indiana Jones, my Luke Skywalker,
    Michael Jordan?
Where is my mission to Mars, my climb up
    Mount Everest?
Me and my friends—we usually just go and get
    some pizza.
On third thought, are we there yet?
Maybe something interesting will happen.

johnny nesbitt

Well, it's me and Mom here,
Waiting for our guest, David.
Minus Dad, of course.
Dad is a big minus any way you look at it.
Mom said the reason they got a divorce
Was that he was married to the store, not her.
She says the *store* should file for divorce
For nonsupport because business is so bad.
And ever since they opened the new supermarket,
It's been even worse, if that's possible.
But Mom said he'd never give up on the store
'Cause that's the only thing he has—
That and the bottle.
If that sounds kinda cold, I'm not apologizing.
But I really do feel sorry for him.
How'd you feel if you had an open house every day
And people would pass your door,
Nod politely, even ask how you're doin',
And head for the fancier place up the block?
Hey, I think I can see the bus coming in now.

david khalil

Before we arrive, they have asked us
To fill out this questionnaire on the bus,
Asking who we are, what we like.
I do not know how to answer exactly.
My father was from Pakistan;
My mother comes from Trinidad;
My brother married a girl from Toronto.
He lives up there now
And complains about the weather all the time.
My sister studied in England;
She married a barrister from Brighton.
I have an aunt from Antigua,
An uncle in Uruguay,
And three cousins who visit from Colombia.
The United Nations lies at the
Roots of my family tree.
How do I know what I am
If there is no family Bible to consult,
Just a family atlas?

melinda kurtz

When I meet Stella
I'd like to tell her
This town's a bore,
And a whole lot more.
It's stone-cold dead here,
Throughout the whole year,
Nothin' to do,
As I'm waitin' for you.
Sure, my heart is full,
With a tractor pull,
It's such a rush,
Spreadin' cornmeal mush.
What a wonderful joy
Knowin' every boy,
This one-horse town
Has beaten me down.
Can't describe the thrill,
Sledding the same ol' hill,
Life has to offer more
Than the general store.
Aw, gee, shucks,
Animal Farm sucks,
I refuse to be caught standing
Forever in Hudson Landing.

 # stella church

When I meet Mel
I got things to tell,
That life in the city
Is not nearly so pretty.
People are stoned and kinda cold there,
Sad faces linger all through the year.
Too much to do,
I'm tellin' you.
My lungs are choked
From soot and smoke,
Crime on the rise,
City life's no prize.
It's such a treat,
Guys see you as meat,
This crazy metro
Has my life in retro.
Please let me stay up here;
I want to see a real live deer.
Let me leave life urban
For places more suburban.
Hey, hot damn,
I'm nowhere, man,
Maybe it's strange,
My new home on the range.

amy sWinton

My mother outmaneuvers Martha Stewart.
She outradiates Rosie O'Donnell.
She is the head of the Ladies Auxiliary at
    First Methodist,
President of the PTA, chair of the Chamber
    of Commerce.
If it's happening in Hudson Landing, she knows
    about it,
Or is responsible for it, or has an objection to it.
For relaxation she makes quilts, which she gives away;
She also makes preserves and donates them to the
    Senior Center.
Look at her standing there, holding the
    welcoming sign,
Feeling personally and singularly responsible for
    this event.
Everyone in town thinks she's so wonderful—
Everyone but me, that is.
I know about her "business trips," she calls them,
Exploring economic opportunities for the town,
    she says.
At a motel, two towns over? Exploring what?
Tell you the whole story when I get the chance,
But right now I see the bus coming, and my mother
    is calling me.
She wants me to stand next to her so she can
    feel proud.
My mother makes beautiful quilts,
Which have won prizes at the county fair.
It's a wonder to see how she covers everything up.

katie fung

My father thinks I am a China star,
Shining brightly in the academic heavens.
He smiles at me, and I smile back
To assure him his sacrifices were worthwhile.
My father left his job, my mother her family,
So I could streak across the sky,
Like some comet blazing across America.
He is convinced I will go to Harvard;
I am not convinced I will graduate on time.
I did not do so well on my last history test
And my English writing remains stiff and awkward.
I am in fear of telling my parents this.
My star has dimmed; my future has paled.
I worry, if I do not enter a good college,
What will I do with the rest of my life?
Will I look up to the night sky
And see nothing but a black void?
Maybe I can stay up here in the country.
There are a lot more stars visible,
Shining brilliantly.

valerie van garp

When I first saw Lolita Rosenbaum,
I simply thought I was going to die.
She leaped off the bus—
Her hair orange,
Her nails black,
Her top short,
Her navel pierced,
Her skirt tight,
Her eyebrow pierced too—
Saw my sign, and screamed,
"Valerie, it's me, it's me!"
I simply wanted to crawl into a hole and die.
"They got any clubs near here,
Anything to do, anything to see?
And where are the good-looking farmer-type studs?"
I simply figured I would die of mortification.
But before I had a chance to say anything, she asked,
"Where your folks,
Split up like mines?
Who needs 'em anyway?
There a bathroom 'round here?
I gotta pee.
You got a cigarette?
Anything stronger?"
I think we're gonna get along just great.

lolita rosenbaum

When I first saw Valerie van Garp,
I thought I was gonna puke.
She just stood there, frozen—
Her hair stiff,
Her nails pink,
Her top long,
Her navel hidden,
Her skirt loose,
Her eyebrow unpierced—
Carrying her sign and saying nothing.
I thought she was some sort of mannequin.
Then *I* said something about clubs,
Anything to see or do, and
Where did all the good-looking dudes hang out.
I couldn't get any reaction out of her.
Then I asked her about her folks,
Told her I had to pee,
And could I bum a cigarette off her.
Then the weirdest thing happened:
She broke into this humongous smile and hugged me.
I think we're gonna get along just great.

brian paxell

My mother drags me to box socials,
Where I have to smile at people I don't like.
I want to go swimming with my friends.
She thinks I should learn social graces.
I want to go off by myself.
She says, "Hermits are usually mentally ill.
Have another portion of potato salad."
I feel my life is a box of

c	school	f
h		a
u		m
r		i
c		l
h	rules	y

One day I'll untie the strings,
Remove the wrapping paper from my soul,
And push against the flaps
That keep me locked inside.
And what's more, I'll never attend
Another box social in my life.
Sorry, Mom.

tommy la blanca

My brother, Anthony, left me holdin' the bag.
For real.
I got probation and a warning from the judge
That if he ever saw me in his court again,
He'd take my Italian ass and send it to
The University of Attica, no joke.
My mama twisted my ear and told me
I'm gonna wind up a good-for-nothin' bum.
My girlfriend dropped me 'cause she says
She didn't wanna be seen with no jailbird,
No matter how cool that looks.
My father thinks I'm a joke,
That I seen *GoodFellas* too many times.
But I ain't no joke; inside, I'm a serious guy.
The edges of my life may be cuttin' me up,
But there is one place where I feel good.
No matter how bad I been, no matter what I done,
The church always forgives me for everything.
I love the whole thing—music, sermon, confession.
Father Boyle lets me stay as long as I like.
He never hurries me; he forgives me.
He makes me feel good inside, peaceful.
You tell anyone this,
I'll bust your head wide open.

jason palmer

The train track
Reaches like a long finger in the night,
Pointing the way back home.
Last week I took a train to the city,
To look at several colleges
That were interested in me.
Each place had more students than people in my town.
Oh, the libraries were impressive, the dorms inviting,
And the people were friendly for the most part,
But not as friendly as folks up here in Hudson,
Where it takes me half an hour to walk up Main Street,
Talking to this friend here and that store owner there.
Jeez, my childhood is on that street.
These people know my name, my family, my history.
The train track stretches to many parts of the world.
But I'm glad it stretches back to Hudson.
You know, I'm nervous about meeting Kwame.
What if we have nothing to talk about
And he takes the next train back home?

kwame richards

I am not a slave on the Niger.
I do not chop sugarcane in Cuba.
I refuse to work the docks in New Orleans.
I am not a bellman, porter, dishwasher, janitor—
Anymore.
I am a proud black man,
With a future grander than the Nile.
I am a good son, good student, good citizen,
Mindful of my past but not bound to it.
Don't tell me to
Go out for the high school basketball team,
As if that's the only thing I can do.
Don't pull my chain by telling me
I've got some serious moves to the hole,
As if that's the best thing I can do.
I hope Jason, the guy I'm staying with,
Does not see me only in terms of black and white.
I really hope he is color-blind.

buddy erikson

My father is the town constable,
And I feel like I'm on parole.
I must bring home the best grades
Even though I am not the best student.
I must be a star member of the football team
Even though I really can't stand the sport.
My brother escaped into the army,
And one day I want to follow him,
Getting as far away from my father
As the circumference of the world will allow.
That's why I broke up with Becky;
I want no strings tying me to this town.
My brother and I used to play tennis;
The sweet sound of shots,
The soft scuffle of sneakers
Linked us as partners for life.
I miss my brother a lot;
We didn't have enough time together.
It will have to serve, though, until I see him again.
Right now I'm waiting for the bus from the city.
I wonder if this kid, Anthony, likes having a
    twin brother.
I know I would.

anthony la blanca

Friday nights I cruise the avenue,
Lookin' for whaddya think?
Saturday nights I cruise the avenue again,
Lookin' for what I missed the first time.
You think they do the same thing up here?
Maybe that's why they call their cars pickup trucks.
They ain't got what I got—
A Mustang 5.0 with mag wheels,
Leather interior so the girls can slide over,
A 300-watt Pioneer system with a ten-CD changer in
    the trunk,
And a special hiding place where I stash the booze.
And I gotta go upstate in a cheese bus?
Hope none of my friends see me in that.
I wouldn't be goin' on this trip
If my car wasn't in the shop.
But, hey, give the girls a rest one weekend.
I'll be back on the avenue soon,
Puttin' my car and my body into overdrive.

becky beauclaire

After Buddy Erikson, my one true love,
There haven't been too many others.
The guys I meet want one thing only,
And when they don't get it,
They sulk and crawl away like beaten puppies.
I like it that way now;
I am my own best company, or so I thought,
Until I realized I was turnin' into a very boring person.
So I signed up to have an exchange student.
Angie will be here in a few minutes—
I hope she's nice—it might be fun, I don't know.
I need a new friend, one who won't make demands
And one who will leave after a couple of days.
My parents ask why I leave the porch light on.
I leave it on for Buddy.
He might come back to me one day,
When he realizes he ain't gonna find nobody better.

 # angie perry

I'm sittin' on the bus,
Hearin' people complain about
Parents who yell at them,
Brothers who pick on them,
Sisters who steal from them,
Grandparents who nag at them.
I'm sittin' on the bus,
Hearin' people complain about
Teachers who fail them,
Counselors who ignore them,
Friends who ditch them,
Bosses who cheat them,
And I wonder how spoiled they can be—
These students who have more money than God,
These students who have their own cars,
These students who have Mommy and Daddy
Wiping their noses,
Picking up their rooms,
Saving for their futures.
Maybe I'm goin' on this trip
To rent a family, at least for the weekend.
I think I would like for once in my life
To experience the luxury of complaint.

harlan jones,
editor, hudson valley sentinel

Editor's Note

Dear Hunters,

As we approach another hunting season, we should be mindful to avoid the embarrassment—no, the tragedy—we suffered last year when a couple of wanna-be hunters mistook a cow for a buck and shot the poor animal dead. Mr. Ray Loudermilk, owner of the deceased cow, promises he will personally instruct any city slicker as to the biological differences between the two species.

Inside this week's issue:

what dance, where?

melinda kurtz

Thank you for the chair, Miss Carter.
Your store is so lovely.
This is my new friend, Stella.
I'm not taking up too much room, am I?
I'm a little tired from all that walking.
It's his first Christmas, you know.
I wanted him to get a sense
Of all the music, lights, and smells.
Isn't that right, my little flower?
Stop your kicking, we'll be going in just a minute.
You don't have to tell me what you want.
I already know what it is.
I'm just gonna buy you everything I can.
Miss Carter, how much do I got in my account?
Thanks.
When's the baby due?
Next month, near the twenty-fifth.
I couldn't wait so many months.
To show him his first Christmas.
Come on, Stella, let's go.
I can't wait to get out on that floor.

stella church

Before the dance Melinda took me to her favorite store.
It wasn't the Gap, Banana Republic, or Aeropostale.
It was a kind of store I never seen before.
"This is our Christmas store," she said.
When I didn't understand, she explained,
"It's open all year 'round, like a bank,
And you make deposits on the stuff you see here.
And by the time Christmas rolls around
Your tree has lotsa presents underneath."
I stared openmouthed at the
Angels, red boxes, and frosted windows.
"You don't have these in the city?" she asked, smiling.
"This store gets me through the rough times."
When we left, carols trailing us, I asked
Whether she was in a condition to go to a dance.
"The kid loves it," she said.
"You should see how he jumps around.
Isn't that store simply beautiful?"

oliver nesbitt, town board member no. 1
johnny nesbitt

What dance, where?
You didn't tell me about any dance.
I told you before, didn't I?
I need you to work the store late tonight.
Something's come up, and I gotta take care of it.
That's right, run off,
Run off to your stupid little dance.
Leave me in the lurch,
Just like your mother did.
That's right, get out of here.
I'll take care of everything.
Bad enough I'm being killed
By the new supermarket.
I can't even pay my bills,
But what do you care?
You do what you wanna do anyway.
Everyone's leaving me,
So you might as well also.
That's right, go,
Go, what do I need you for?
I'll just take care of business by myself.

What business, where?
Dad, you're just goin' out to get drunk again.

valerie van garp

Who the hell does she think she is?
Just because her father's the manager
Of the biggest store in town,
She thinks she can just breeze in and take over,
Toss her golden hair like some sort of princess?
I see the way the boys look at her.
They cover the front of their pants with their books.
They walk around practically drooling at her.
If she said, "Jump," they would say, "How high?"
If she said, "Jump in the lake," there would be
    mass suicide.
I saw it with my own two eyes.
Me and Johnny were walking up toward the school.
He saw her, and his head whipped around.
"Do you need a lawyer?" I asked.
"For what?" he said, still looking.
"For the whiplash injury you just suffered."
I swear I could kill Kristen Clarke.
Who the hell does she think she is?

annie gardiner, teacher, hudson landing central high school

My mother believes in total honesty.
She has an opinion about everything:
About the men I date,
About the men I should date,
Not that there is much to choose from around here.
On my relationships:
All men cheat;
It's just a matter of when, with whom,
And can they get away with it.
On my career:
You're gonna wind up an old-maid schoolteacher.
How can you stand those kids all day long?
Why do you spend your Friday nights at football games
    or dances?
On my appearance:
Why don't you wear more makeup?
Why don't you cut your hair?
Why don't you fix yourself up?
On a need-to-know basis, my mother believes
I need to know everything.
My mother believes in total honesty.
I wish she were a little more dishonest.

john erikson, town constable

Mr. Ziegel, Annie,
I just want to remind you,
The dance has to be over by eleven.
That's cute, Annie:
"Even Cinderella had until twelve."
But you know the ordinance, so eleven o'clock it is.
I'm sorry, Mr. Ziegel, okay, Alan.
I know in the city dances don't even *start* before eleven,
But this is a go-to-bed-early, get-up-early town,
And I see no reason to change things,
Even for something this special.
The kids can have fun earlier, that's all.
You'll find we're a good, peaceful, and quiet town,
And that's because people 'round here obey the rules.
Nothing out of the ordinary ever happens.
People just go about their normal routine,
Minding their own business.
You have a good time, you hear?

annie gardiner, teacher,
hudson landing central high school

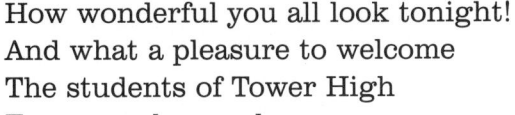

How wonderful you all look tonight!
And what a pleasure to welcome
The students of Tower High
To our exchange dance.
You've certainly come a long way,
And I hope the bus journey hasn't tired you out
    too much.
We have good music and good food,
Courtesy of Ned Clarke, manager of the Grand
    Royale Supermarket,
Which just opened up here in town.
So to get things rolling,
Will our town hosts please line up next to our
    city guests?

Jason Palmer	Kwame Richards
Buddy Erikson	Anthony LaBlanca
Brian Paxell	Tommy LaBlanca
Valerie van Garp	Lolita Rosenbaum
Melinda Kurtz	Stella Church
Kristen Clarke	Cookie Maldonado
Becky Beauclaire	Angie Perry
Aaron Loudermilk	Michael Perrin
Johnny Nesbitt	David Khalil
Amy Swinton	Katie Fung

Tonight promises to be a perfect night.
So just kick back and enjoy yourself.
And may you remember this night for a long, long
    time.

 # kwame richards

 **jason palmer**

When I was in the ninth grade,
We read *Romeo and Juliet.*
I was fourteen;
Romeo was fourteen;
Juliet was thirteen.
The whole world was fourteen then,
And I couldn't understand for the life of me
What the fuss was all about.
I mean, there were other girls at the party.
He didn't have to break his neck on the balcony,
And what's up with this marriage business so quickly?
Now, at seventeen, I understand it is possible
To see a girl across the dance floor,
To get caught in a moment's rush
And feel now what Romeo felt then, that
"I never saw true beauty till this night."
Jason (or are you my friend Mercutio?),
Who is that girl, what is her name?
I must go across the floor,
Across the universe, and meet her,
Though I probably could not tell you why.
Love, it seems, is not as simple as
Black and white.

angie perry becky beauclaire

"You eat like that all the time?"
 "Sure, why not? When I go home, that is."
"Why wouldn't you want to go home?"
 "I'd have to talk to my parents then."
"And that's bad because?"
 "You don't have to live with them.
 What's the city like?"
"It's cool, lots to do,
Especially at night."
 "You'll show me?"
"It'll be my pleasure."
 "Who's that guy? He's cute."
"In the corner?"
 "Yeah."
"Anthony, or Tommy, they're twins.
Anthony, I think, but leave it alone."
 "Why?"
"He's a player, you know the type."
 "I sure do, all men suck, but introduce me,
 I'll take my chances."

anthony la blanca

buddy erikson

Boy, this schmuck's a loser; he never says a word.
    Boy, I sure got stuck; this guy doesn't shut up.

"A high school dance, you gotta be kiddin'.
Any clubs around here?
Hey, buddy boy, any sweet ladies here at the dance?
How are they, easy?
I mean easy to talk to, no disrespect intended."
    "None taken."
"I hear your father's a cop; that must be a trip."
    "It's okay."
"He must see a lotta blood."
    "Nope."
"You always talk so much?"
    "Not often."
"I guess that's why the town's so quiet."
    "Reckon."
"What does *reckon* mean? Talk Eng— Wait a sec.
Who's that bomb that just walked in?"
    "Kristen."
"What can you tell me about her?"
    "Not much."

david khalil johnny nesbitt

My host, Johnny, seems nice enough,
But he is always joking and making fun of people.
He does not treat his parents,
Particularly his father, with respect,
For when I ask him what does his father do, he says,
"He is usually too drunk to do anything,"
And then he laughs as if it were a big joke.
But I do not think he laughs inside.
I think his heart is full of pain.
When he thinks no one is looking,
He sneaks a drink from a small bottle he carries.
I am surprised the teachers do not see it,
And I am much ashamed to mention it to them.
I know my father, if he were alive,
Would be most angry to see this kind of behavior.
Johnny tells me after this dance he plans to take
    his car,
Go to the next town, where there is no curfew,
Where the bartender will wink at his ID,
Where he can drink all night long, would I like
    to come?
As his guest, do I report him to our teachers,
Or must I cover my eyes while he drives himself
    to drink?

cookie maldonado

kristen clarke

Girl, you think you're fat?
You think you've put on a few pounds?
Girl, who's been lyin' to you?
You really believe you're ugly?
You really believe you're too tall?
Girl, who's been tellin' you stories?
I *wish* I could look like you,
But that ain't gonna happen.
I *wish* I could catch the boys' attention,
But that ain't gonna happen neither.
What you mean too much attention?
Ain't no such thing as too much attention.
I swear you could be a model, no kidding.
What do you mean, no way?
You wanna tell me something?
A secret?
In the ladies' room?
What's it about?
Yes, I am willing to hold the horses.
Where are they?
Do I think you're pretty?
What's the matter with you, girl?

brian paxell
tommy la blanca

Hey, Tommy, don't this dance suck?
It's for kids, you think?
Everyone pretending to be nice and proper
For two whole days, wow.
Then they go back to their same nasty selves.
Man, I'm tired of this town.
It's getting so you can't even breathe 'round here
Without breaking some ordinance or something.
The chicks in town are either virgins or knocked up.
See that girl Melinda there?
Ready to pop in a month or so, I tell you.
Your girls look strange altogether.
What's up with that Lolita chick? She's weird.
Hey, I know what, got my twenty-two in the back of
    my pickup,
Say we go by the lake and target shoot.
I can set up some cans by the headlights.
Come on, let's go, you know anything about guns?
I just feel like shooting something,
Or someone.

 # lolita rosenbaum
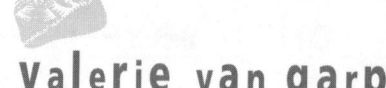 **valerie van garp**

Val, let me tell you about the city.
Oh, it's so cool.
Sometimes, when I'm out clubbing,
I don't even know the boy I'm dancing with.
I got so many boyfriends they drip off me like sweat.
I get into so many clubs even the bouncers say,
"Lolita, honey, you should have
A permanent stamp on your hand."
And when I go shopping with my girlfriends,
There ain't nothing that don't look good on me.
And in school?
Well, in school, I crack everyone up.
I can make someone laugh by just looking at them,
Know what I'm saying?
Everybody knows me;
Everybody loves me.
I rule.
Do you understand what I'm talking about?
Not quite?
You're being much too polite, you know.
Sometimes I feel I'm just full of crap.

melinda kurtz  stella church

Oh, this is so lovely.
I can't believe how they fixed up the gym.
The flowers are pink and blue—
Ironic, don't you think?
Dance with me, Stella,
Dance with me before the music stops.
I don't want it to stop.
Don't worry, I'm not gay or bi.
I just don't want any boy touching me right now,
Isn't the music gr—
Oh, my God, not now,
Please not now, it's too early.
Oh, my stomach.
Please don't tell Ms. G.
I don't want to spoil anyone's fun.
I'm not feeling up for a whole lot of questions either.
Stella, help me!
Take my arm; you have to get me to Dr. Hicks's.
It's just up the road.
Don't look scared; it'll be all right.
Hurry, I don't wanna have this kid in the bathroom.

 **amy swinton**  **katie fung**

See this camera?
My mother is making me
Take pictures of the dance tonight,
So she can hang the prints on her office wall,
Proof positive this event was her own doing.
One day I'll leave Hudson Landing,
Go to the city and become a professional photographer.
She'll be lucky if she gets a postcard from me.
Hang with me while I shoot a quick roll,
And then I'm going to show you something spectacular.
Grab your coat, girl, we're going down by the lake.
If we're lucky, we can frame an animal or two.
"The woods are lovely, dark and deep,"
And I have pictures to shoot 'fore I sleep.
You're thinking there is not enough light, right?
You're wrong, my camera can see everything.
So come outside and taste the beautiful outdoors.
I'd like to show you this beautiful starlit night
In its proper focus.

aaron loudermilk

michael perrin

Great dance, wasn't it?
Yeah, I know it's early,
But we got a curfew in this town that sucks,
And if you break it, TC Erikson
Throws you in the slammer for a few hours.
Forget that, is that girl Lolita wild or what?
I think I'd like her to show me around when we
    visit you.
You came up with some fine-looking women,
Although you gotta admit Kristen got them all beat.
Your guy, Kwame, was sweating her all evening.
Don't see 'em now.
Maybe they're somewhere doin' it.
I see Ms. Gardiner talking with your teacher, what's
    his name?
Think they're getting cozy? Could happen.
She could use some relaxation; she's stressed.
Time to go, Michael, I gotta get up early and milk
    the cows.
You ever see the rear end of a cow before?
Didn't think so.
I got some beer in my truck.
You drink?

annie gardiner, teacher, hudson landing central high school

I'm young, but I'm old inside.
I am as old as the historical characters I teach.
I teach but have not lived.
I dream but have not participated.
I look into the faces of my students tonight,
See what a good time they're having,
And wish I were out on the dance floor with them.
I am a hypocrite.
I tell them to explore
While I haven't traveled.
I tell them to stretch
While I haven't moved a muscle.
Look at them in the middle of the dance floor,
Laughing, joking, carrying on,
While I sit on the sidelines
Waiting for Life to ask me to dance.
No, I am not ready;
No, I do not know the steps;
And the music I hear sounds loud and unfamiliar.
Is it time to go already?
I haven't even taken a single step.
Maybe next summer I will go to Italy
And dance the night away under the Roman stars.

alan ziegel, teacher, tower high school

When I was in school myself—
It seems a million years ago—
Dances terrified me:
What to say, where to stand, who to ask.
Tripping over my feet,
Putting my foot in my mouth,
And never feeling quite at ease.
Now, here at this dance,
I can honestly say
It's a treat, not a terror,
Watching everyone enjoying themselves.
I'd like to thank the students of
Hudson Landing Central High School
For hosting this dance.
And I'd like to thank Ms. Gardiner
For making us feel quite at home.
We'll say good night now.
Tomorrow is a big day.
Everyone here?
Who's missing?
No, I don't know where he is.
Anyone seen Kwame?

cookie maldonado

Kristen, Kristen,
Where are you?
You were here a minute ago.
Where'd you go?
Are they serious with this curfew?
Shoot, I ain't had a curfew since I was in junior high.
My mom trusts me day or night,
And a few hours one way or another
Ain't gonna make a whole lot of difference.
People can get preggo day or night.
Kristen, just lose Kwame.
You've been dancing with him all evening.
We can go back to your house,
Sit in front of the fireplace,
Have your dad make us hot chocolate,
And stay up all night and talk.
Girl, where are you?
Did you go off with him?
I don't think he's your type.

who killed kristen clarke?

john erikson, town constable

Yes?
Yes, Ned.
Slow down.
What?
Where?
When?
Wearing?
With whom?
Slow down, Ned.
We'll find her.
At a friend's likely.
One of the boys from the city?
The high school exchange group?
Which kid?
The black one?
Which black one?
That one?
We'll talk to him.
Sure, you bet.
Keep calm, Ned.
Everything'll be all right.

# ned m. clarke, manager,
grande royale supermarket

Don't tell me to calm down.
Just because I haven't lived in this town
For two centuries, I gotta wait?
Why isn't he out right now looking for her?
Does he have a daughter?
Does he wait for the key in the door at night?
When I dropped them off at the dance,
Her, and that girl from the city, Cookie,
I told them to come directly home afterward,
Not to talk to anyone, not to go with anyone.
So what does my wonderful daughter do?
She rolls her eyes, sees that big black boy,
The one that looks like a basketball player,
And gives him a big hug,
Right in front of my eyes,
Right in front of everyone.
I should have grabbed her and dragged her home.
Just wait till she gets home;
I'll listen to her calmly,
Ask her a couple of questions,
Make sure she's all right,
And then I'm gonna kill her.

john erikson, town constable

Guess I'll head over to the school;
The dance should be way over by now.
Don't know what Ned Clarke is getting so riled about.
Kids are probably just talking, that's all.
I used to like going to dances,
When it wasn't work,
When I was in high school,
When the moon was as bright as it is tonight.
I met my wife, Jennie, over at Edgemont,
At a high school dance, my junior year.
Jennie once told me,
She knew when she first met me at the dance,
We were going to be married.
She saw a future for us.
She saw a family for us.
She saw me as her dance partner for life.
She didn't see the car that hit her four years ago,
Killing her instantly and me slowly.
She didn't see it coming at all.
I'm sure Ned's kid is all right.
Wonder if they remembered to turn off the lights in
the gym.

ned m. clarke, manager,
grande royale supermarket

Yes, I know one day you'll leave for college,
Returning only occasionally.
Yes, I know one day you'll leave for another town,
Writing only sporadically.
Yes, I know you'll have a new name,
Hyphenating your two last names.
Yes, I know one day you'll bear children,
Sending me snapshots infrequently.
But until that day comes, sweetheart,
Until you walk out that door
And into your new life,
You are my baby, no matter
How tall, how rude, how grown-up you are,
No matter how much distance
You try to put between us.
I remember the times you used to sit in my lap,
Not so long ago, was it, baby doll?
Come on, honey, it's late—
Way past curfew, yours and the town's.
Won't you put the key in the lock,
Try to sneak upstairs,
So I can turn over and go to sleep,
Knowing that you are home, sweet home?

john erikson, town constable
dr. adolphus hicks,

town board member no. 4

Evening, Doc.
Beautiful night, ain't it?
Moon looks like a dinner plate.
You didn't, by any chance,
See Ned Clarke's girl, did you?
Probably nothin' to worry about.
Decided to come up here first,
'Cause I hear she takes to the road sometimes.
Thought she and a city kid could be out explorin'.
Didn't see 'em, huh?
Well, I guess I'll be heading to the gym.
Maybe they're still hanging 'round there.

 Evening, John,
 It *is* a beautiful night.
 Don't know when it's been so bright.
 Nope, didn't see her.
 Pretty girl, isn't she?
 Oh, you should know,
 Melinda Kurtz had a baby,
 'Bout an hour ago.
 Mother and daughter are doing just fine.
 You'll excuse me, John,
 I've got to make a call
 And see to my new patients.

george and emily gibson

Honey, I know you're tired,
But everything will be all right.
How many agencies have we been to?
How many ads have we placed?
How many calls have we received?
And didn't we even travel out of the country once
Because some lawyer knew somebody who
  knew somebody?
There's nothing wrong with this.
We're just eliminating the middleman.
We're just avoiding the bureaucratic red tape.
What's wrong? We're providing a good home,
Better than any teenager could,
Better than any foster care could.
Look at Frank and Marilyn Langer down the block.
Look at their beautiful baby,
And tell me they made a mistake.
I'm nervous too, honey, waiting for the phone to ring.
Dr. Hicks promised he'd call back in thirty minutes.
I believe he is a good man, a man of his word.
Sure, I'll hold you tight.
It'll be all right, you'll see.

brian paxell

Did I see her at the dance?
Of course I did; everyone did.
Hard not to notice her.
She was wearing a white dress.
Who did she leave with?
Don't remember, maybe the black guy, I don't know.
When I saw her, she was with him.
The tall black guy in city clothes,
You know, hip-hop, baggy pants, turned-around hat.
She was right out there, dancing real close.
How long she know the guy, half an hour?
Good thing there were people on the floor or
In another few minutes
They would have been dancing horizontally.
Kristen is the most beautiful girl in town.
She has the pick of any guy she wants.
And believe me, she's picked quite a few of them.
People say she went out with half the football team,
Exploring different positions, you might say.
But I'm not one to spread any gossip.
I just wish she had picked me to go home with.
No, I didn't see who she left with.
Could have been anyone.

becky beauclaire

Was who at the dance?
Kristen?
I don't talk to that bitch anymore.
I'm tryin' to get Buddy to like me again,
Talkin' to him near the dance floor,
Only I can't hear a damn thing
'Cause the music's pumped up so loud.
I'm tryin' to be all friendly-like,
When Kristen walks into the room,
Or rather, slithers, 'cause her dress is so tight.
Buddy takes one good look at her,
And I swear his eyeballs pop out of his head.
I try and steer him
Over to the food table, away from her.
She's missin'?
I didn't see Buddy neither.
Ain't that cute?
Maybe they're together, I don't know.
Personally I couldn't care less.

investigating I: john erikson, town constable

"I didn't see her all night."
"I couldn't take my eyes offa her."
                    "She left with the black guy."
        "I think she went with that girl Cookie."
"Melinda left early,
I don't think she was feeling well."
                    "Johnny Nesbitt's not here,
                    Probably drunk somewheres."
"Sorry to bother you, Mrs. Swinton.
Is your daughter home?"
                    "Buddy looked angry,
                    Like he was gonna explode."
"Jason's not here.
I saw him leave early."
                    "TC Erikson,
                    They all went back home."
"I didn't see her.
Didn't she go back at curfew?"
                    "Why do you wish to talk to me?
                    Is it about the drinking?"
"I'm hung over,
I don't know nothin'."
                    "No, I didn't see her.
                    Maybe her father picked her up."

investigating II: john erikson,
town constable

So what do I have?
Not much, not much at all.
A town on edge,
A list that's getting me nowhere:

Father	hysterical, overprotective
Brian Paxell	crush on her, left early
Johnny Nesbitt	crush on her, out drinking
Becky Beauclaire	obviously jealous
Valerie van Garp	ditto
Cookie Maldonado	one of the last to see her
Yvette Rondeau	jilted girlfriend, out of town
Penny Marsden	worked with Kristen Clarke, hated her
The Dropout	worked with Kristen Clarke, desired her
Anthony LaBlanca	wanted to meet her
Amy Swinton	left early
Aaron Loudermilk	left early, may be drinking
The Drifter	motorcycle hasn't been seen lately

Then, of course, there is someone at the top of the list.
How many people told me he danced with her?
How many people told me he left with her?
Every finger points to him.
You can't ignore what good townspeople say,
I gotta think he's the one,
The one that stands out in a crowd,
The one that has given us all a black eye.
Yeah, Joe, speak louder,
Must be a poor connection, what is it?
I'll be right down, you just stay put.

along main street

Did you hear 'bout the dance?
    I heard.
There was a lot of drinking going on.
    More than that.
There was a near riot.
    The TC had to call in the state troopers.
Three people are missing.
    Five, six maybe.
Two people got hurt.
    Four.
City kids brought in drugs.
    Doc Hicks is treating them now.
That Clarke girl wore practically nothing.
    Stripped, from what they say.
Ms. Gardiner got drunk with that city teacher fellow.
    Drove over to the next town.
Be a long time 'fore there's another dance.
    A long time.
And that's not the half of it.
    I bet.
Keep this under your hat, no sense spreading stories.
    You bet.

 # kwame richards

Ja...
Son,...
That...
You?...
What...
Happened?...
Where...
Am...
I?...
The...
Other...
Boat,...
Other...
Boat....
Where's...
Kristen?...
Other boat....
Is...
She...
All...
Right?...
Help...
Me,...
Please.

kwame richards

What's up with this?
My arm hurts like hell.
I think the cop broke it
Before he threw me in here.
All I know is I was hanging with Jason,
Waiting to go see the town constable,
When this cop
Pulled up in his cruiser and
Asked if I was Kwame Richards,
And before I knew it,
He grabbed my arm and dragged my butt
Down to this two-bit jail.
I kept asking, "What did I do?
    What did I do?"
He kept saying, "Shut up, city boy,
    You know what you did—
    That poor girl."
"What girl, what girl are you talking about?"
He told me to just shut up.
Please, go get Mr. Ziegel.
I didn't do anything,
I swear it.

alan ziegel, teacher, tower high school

Officer Erikson?
Excuse me, Town Constable Erikson,
With all due respect, sir,
I'd like to know why
You're holding my student Kwame Richards.
What's he supposed to have done?
You've got to be joking—
Suspicion of murder?
Kwame wouldn't hurt a fly.
Sure, he was at the dance.
So were a lot of other people.
What's that prove?
Have you let him call his parents?
Have you let him consult a lawyer?
Have you charged him with a crime?
What do you mean, "I'm only questioning him"?
What's that mean?
Is it because he's from the city?
Is it because he speaks differently?
I hope your reason for holding him
Is more than just skin-deep.
Can I see him now?

kwame richards

Mr. Ziegel, you know me, you taught me,
I didn't do it,
I swear I didn't do it.
Did I see her?
Did I speak to her?
Did I think she was hot?
Did I dance with her?
Yes, yes, yes, and yes.
Did I sweet-talk her?
Did I leave with her?
Did I row out in the boat with her?
Did I kiss her?
Yes, yes, yes, and yes.
Did I kill her?
Nooooooo!
They got me here 'cause I'm black, right?
They want to pin this on me, don't they?
I swear on my mother's life I didn't kill her.
You believe me, don't you?
I'm scared, Mr. Ziegel.
Can I call my mom?
You think I need a lawyer?

 # angie perry

Mr. Z., what do you mean, I can't see him?
He's my buddy, my pal, my homeboy.
When the kids at school called me a weirdo,
He took me home,
Where his mom fixed me up
With the best meal I ever had.
Ain't no way he drowned that girl.
Sure, maybe he was putting a move on her; so what?
Shoot, man, that's just hormones.
Since when is tryin' to get laid a crime?
But killing her, tossin' her out of a boat?
No way that happened, I know.
He once wrote me a poem that said,
"Angie, for the angel
Who will one day fly home."
He believed in me, and I believe in him.
Mr. Z., I'm not movin' from this spot,
Not until I can see him.
Man, what they're doin' to him is an American tragedy.

oliver nesbitt, town board member no. 1

Heard you got him locked up, John.
Good thing too
'Cause the way I heard it
Some people in town were ready
To take care of him, know what I mean?
I heard the poor girl didn't even have a chance.
Such a sweet girl.
He must've took her out in one of them boats by
    the dock,
And when she wouldn't give him nothin',
The bastard strangled her and threw her
    body overboard.
He was probably high on speed or pot or
Whatever these kinds of kids take nowadays.
At least that's what I heard.
It's all over town, John.
You gonna keep him here
Or transfer him over to Saratoga?

john erikson, town constable

Look, I can hold the boy for twenty-four hours,
No more than that, Ollie,
But then I gotta charge him or let him go.
I don't care what you heard.
He's stayin' put till I find answers to some questions.

over

Questions

all   the

place.

Twenty-four hours:
Time enough to change a life forever,
His
And
Mine.
You better go, Ollie. I got work to do.

coffee shop talk

Of course he did it.
You have any doubts?
What'd you expect?
Those kinda kids come up,
And before you can blink an eye,
There's all kinds of trouble.
Trial?
We don't need no trial.
It's simple, Mac,
The city kids don't come up,
She ain't killed.
They do come up,
And they find her floating in the lake.
I don't know why John's waitin',
What's that kid gonna say?
She just fell outta the boat and drowned?
I'd shoot the bastard and be done with it.
You have any doubts?
Of course he did it.

edith fromer, town board member no. 3

Do I have any doubts?
Of course I do.
Now, I don't know what happened.
I wasn't out there on the lake,
But the point is, neither were you!
Where is it written in stone that he's guilty?
I say the poor boy is entitled to
A smart lawyer,
A good judge,
And a fair trial.
Pete, what are you going to do,
Swing a rope across a tree branch?
Ed, what are you going to do,
Drag him from the back of your pickup?
Cal, what are you going to do,
Take him out back and shoot him?
I know the whole town's hurting.
I know the whole town'll take a beating for this,
But that doesn't mean we have to run around
Like chickens without their heads.
We aren't animals, no doubt about it.

henry maddox, pastor,
new deliverence church

I've come down to the jail to see
If the poor boy wishes some spiritual guidance.
Yes, John, I know we're not executing him,
Yet he might feel the need to lay open his heart
And remove the terrible burden from his soul.
Do I think he's guilty?
We are all "sinners in the hands of an angry God,"
But it is not for me to say.
Only the good Lord knows for sure.
Yes, John, and a jury would too.
I have heard the talk in the town,
How they blame the board for letting those kids
    come up,
How they blame Annie Gardiner for organizing the
    weekend,
How they blame "poor neighborhoods"—code
    words, I think.
But I say, "Let he without sin cast the first stone."
Believe me, in this town no stones should be
    thrown at all.
If you need me, John, just call up the store.
I got a few VCRs to fix, winter's comin' soon.

 john erikson, town constable

I don't know if we're speaking the same language,
So let me try to understand what you're saying.
You were on the lake after midnight, right?
After the dance and certainly after the town curfew.
You know about our curfew laws, don't you, son?
You just happened to be on the lake with
    Kristen Clarke,
A girl you had just met, "instant chemistry,"
    your words.
You just happened to see another boat row toward you.
You don't recognize the person in that boat.
He's wearing a mask; you think it's a joke
    or something.
He knocks you over the head with some sort of
    blunt object,
And just before you lose consciousness, you hear
    Kristen scream.
Then, when you wake up,
Kristen is gone, the man is gone, the boat is gone,
And the reason you don't report this right away is...?
Gotta tell you, son, I'm having a little trouble with
    your story.
You want to go over it again for me?
And this time slow down a bit.
We got all the time in the world.

john erikson, town constable

Son,
Listen, I have a boy of my own,
And I'm speaking to you like I'd speak to him.
Seems to me there are a lot of maybes around here.
Maybe you were drinking,
Maybe it was an accident,
Maybe things just got out of hand.
I don't know, I wasn't there,
But you were, so tell me,
What time did you get to the dance?
What time did you leave it?
And what time were you on the lake?
"I don't know exactly" is not exactly what I'm
    looking for.
What I want, son, is for you to step up,
Stand up, and be a man, admit you did it.
You'll feel a whole lot better once you do, you know.
You'll feel like a rock has been lifted off of you,
    I guarantee.
Like I say, I'm speaking to you like I'd speak to my
    own son.
You have anything you want to tell me?
Nothing?
You're asking me about *my* son, what he'd do?
He doesn't speak to me either.

along main street II

Can you believe it?
　　Oh, it's terrible.
　　　　The worst news imaginable.
　　　　　Poor Mr. Clarke.
　　　　　　　Maybe he shouldn't have moved up here.
　　　　　　　Think he'll close the Royale?
　　　　　　　　Can't do that, people'll starve.
　　　　　　　　His only child.
　　　　　　　　What a shame.
　　　　　　　　　She was so sweet.
　　　　　　　　Not what I heard.
　　　　　　　You go on, Phyllis.
　　　　　　I heard she slept around.
　　　　　No, that can't be true.
　　　　All over 'em, like glue.
　　　Where did you hear that?
　　Kidding me? Everyone knows.
　I didn't hear no such thing.
You're about the only one.

dr. adolphus hicks,
town board member no. 4

The boy?
Nothing serious, a sprained wrist
And a bruise on the side of his head I can't account for.
The girl?
Strangled by someone incompetent,
Inexperienced, or both.
The boy and girl together?
I can't tell.
There's something else, John.
She was pregnant—about three months.
I'd like that kept secret if you don't mind.
No sense giving her father more grief than necessary.
I knew about the pregnancy; she was my patient.
I knew all about her—the rumors, the facts,
And the gossip vultures,
Who pick on the living
And feast on the dead.
All I wish to say is that
Kristen Clarke was a beautiful, loving girl,
Who did not find a home in our town.

amy swinton
john erikson, town constable

TC Erikson?
Hope I'm not bothering you,
It's just that me and Katie were
By the shore last night.
The moon was full,
And I thought I heard the ducks scream.
Only maybe it wasn't the ducks.
It was people in two boats, I think.
I tried to take a picture with my telephoto lens.
Is that Kristen?
Is that the black guy from the dance?
And there was another man.
I couldn't see his face,
But he had on this crazy hat.
See, look at this; sorry it's not too clear.
Will this picture help you,
Or is it just a shot in the dark?

   Wait a second.
   I know that hat!
   I see that hat practically every day in town.

john erikson, town constable

You hear on the news whenever they catch a murderer,
"He'd never hurt anyone,"
"I talked to him just last week,"
"He generally kept to himself."
Oliver, we weren't close friends, but I knew you.
Everyone in town knew you—for years.
You paid your taxes
And said good morning to the folks along Main Street.
Sure, you had your troubles—
We all knew about your drinking—
But even in a small town nobody escapes.
Picket fences hide pain and
Rolling hills obscure rage,
And sometimes desperation may not be so quiet.
But murder, Oliver, the taking of life?
I have seen larceny, petty and grand.
I have seen people lose everything, in fire and flood.
I have seen crime, but nothing like this.
And when they ask me about you on the evening news,
All I will be able to say is
"He generally kept to himself."
It can't be you, Oliver, can it?

 **oliver nesbitt,** town board member no. 1

John, you want to know why?
There are quite a few whys, I suppose.
Why does my ex-wife hate me?
Why does my son not talk to me?
Why does my empty store mock me?
I am stuck to my miserable business,
Ball and chain,
A prisoner of my own failure.
I was on the lake fishing and drinking,
More drinking than fishing,
And I saw the two of them, you know,
Goin' at it hot and heavy.
And I thought, Why is she so young?
Why is he so lucky?
Why do they have everything and
I got nothin' 'cept my boat and my bottle?
It came to me then:
Kill her, and the Royale would close.
Blame him, and our town would remain pure.
Why can't my life be the way it used to be,
When my store and my hopes were new
And nobody from the outside bothered me?
John, you remember the Christmases we had
When everything was simple,
When everything was white?

john erikson, town constable

Kwame, you can go home now.
It wasn't you.
You can leave as soon as you want to.
It wasn't you.
You're welcome to come back soon.
It wasn't you.
It was
The open window,
The clothesline,
The telephone wire,
The Breakfast Stop,
All manner of talk.
It was
The fiction as fact,
The rumor as gospel,
The supposition as statement,
The tale as truth,
All manner of lies.
Kwame, you aren't guilty of anything.
We are.

 # kwame richards

I can go home now?
I can take the bus back to the city,
Like nothing happened,
Like, oops, you're sorry you gave me a speeding ticket,
Like, oops, it was just a minor slipup,
Like, oops, her body wound up floating in the lake?
I can go home now?
With what?
With the memory
That my actions contributed to her death?
With the memory
That you treated me like dirt?
With the memory
That you had me guilty until proven innocent?
Let me ask you something:
The fact that I am black
Had nothing to do with your beliefs?
The fact that I am from the city
Had nothing to do with your assumptions?
Would the same thing have happened if I was white?
Would the same thing have happened if I lived here?
I can go home now?
I can't wait.

harlan jones,

editor, *hudson valley sentinel*

Editorial

One death,
One life:
On the face of it, an even trade,
No?
No, a thousand times over.
The circle of life may be a joyous song for some,
But it does not roll smoothly.
It bounces; it leaps,
Whimsically, arbitrarily,
Crushing some hopes here,
Raising other hopes there.
In greed a life was taken,
In joy a life was given,
But now both are exposed
In the glare of the media's spotlight.
Outsiders have invaded,
Searching under each rock
For a grain of information.
We will never be as we were,
Innocent as we once were.
We will never be just Hudson Landing.
But "that town," the one that heard the cry of
Birth and death on the same moonlit night,
The one that did not take care of its children.

jolene hanks, owner, hudson hardware

We knew about
    The stories that hover over this town like a fog,
    The tales in and out of school,
    And the romances, past and present.
We knew about
    Who dreams, who cries,
    Who lives, who dies,
    And who drinks, who sighs.
We knew about
    Kristen Clarke's carryings-on,
    Johnny Nesbitt's secret drinking,
    And Oliver Nesbitt's divorce and failing store.
We knew even more.
We knew about
    Doc Hicks and his girls,
    The ones who visited him late at night,
    And the strangers who called,
    Never leaving empty-handed.
We knew everything and said nothing.
We knew the murderer and the murdered,
The horrible man and the unfortunate girl,
We knew everything and told no one.
Yes, we knew it all,
Kept it to ourselves,
And turned the other way.

Manager of Grand Royale Set to Leave

Ned M. Clarke, the manager of the Grand Royale Supermarket, announced today that he planned to leave town "by the end of the week."

"I want to thank all the people of Hudson Landing who helped me cope with the loss of my beautiful daughter. I can't express my gratitude for all the wonderful letters I have received," he said.

Three weeks ago Kristen Clarke, seventeen, was found dead in Hudson Lake. After a short investigation Oliver Nesbitt, owner of the Town Store and Deli, was arrested and charged with the crime. He is awaiting trial.

"I would have wanted to continue helping the town to grow," Mr. Clarke said, "but in light of the terrible tragedy I have suffered, it is impossible for me to remain here. I wish the town and its people well."

In response to a growing concern that the Grand Royale will close, Albert Goodson, senior board member, has assured the community that the supermarket will remain open. Assistant Manager Jerry DiPietro will serve as acting manager until a replacement for Mr. Clarke can be found.